# FAMINE AND DROUGHT

NEWS FLASH **HUMAN GEOGRAPHY**

EXPLORE PLANET EARTHS MOST DESTRUCTIVE NATURAL DISASTERS.

# PHOTO CREDITS

©2017
Book Life
King's Lynn
Norfolk PE30 4LS

ISBN: 978-1-78637-102-7

All rights reserved
Printed in Malaysia

A catalogue record for this book
is available from the British Library.

Written by:
Joanna Brundle

Edited by:
Grace Jones

Designed by:
Natalie Carr

# FAMINE AND DROUGHT

# CONTENTS

Words that appear like **this** can be found in the Glossary on page 31.

# WHAT IS A DROUGHT?

A drought is a period of unusually dry weather, lasting long enough to cause water shortages and damage to crops. The most common cause of droughts is a lack of rain, but they can also result from too little snow in areas that depend on melting snow for water.

Shifts in the winds that usually bring rain or changes in ocean currents, which affect the amount of moisture in the air, can also be a cause of droughts.

In areas of drought, people may spend many hours each day searching for water.

An area suffering from drought usually has cracked, dry soil and a cloudless sky. Rivers and lakes **evaporate**, crops **wither** and dust blows in the air. A drought may last for months or even years.

The ground may become so dry that even when it does rain, the water runs off and collects in low-lying areas, causing **flash floods**. Forest fires may result from the heat and high winds.

**An African herdsman, looking for water for his livestock.**

# WHAT IS A FAMINE?

A famine is a severe food shortage, causing many people and animals to die from **starvation**. Drought sometimes causes famine but not always. It may be caused by plant diseases, by crop destruction due to bad weather or **pests**, or by poor farming methods, which rob the soil of its **nutrients**. Sometimes, a country has enough food, but war or **government** problems prevent it from reaching the people.

**A plague of locusts can destroy food crops.**

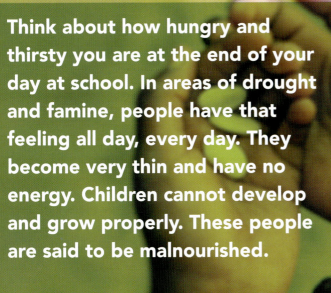

Think about how hungry and thirsty you are at the end of your day at school. In areas of drought and famine, people have that feeling all day, every day. They become very thin and have no energy. Children cannot develop and grow properly. These people are said to be malnourished.

Many people become very ill with diseases like cholera.

Someone who is malnourished often has a swollen stomach, like this.

Volunteers handing out food to hungry people in Ethiopia.

# THE IMPORTANCE OF WATER

Water makes up over two thirds of our bodies and the average human body is thought to contain about thirty-eight litres of water. We lose water when we breathe, sweat or go to the toilet and need to drink around two litres a day to stay healthy. We can survive for about a month without eating, but will die after as few as three days with no water.

**Plants, animals and people – all living things – depend on water for survival.**

**What would sixty-seven pints of milk look like? That's roughly the volume of water in our bodies.**

There is so much water on Earth that our planet appears blue from space, but only around 3% of this water is fresh, drinking water. The rest is too salty for humans to drink. Around two thirds of our fresh water is frozen in **ice caps** and **glaciers**. Most of the remaining third is underground, so fresh water is a valuable and **finite resource**. We mustn't waste a drop!

The longest drought in history affected the Atacama Desert in Chile from 1571–1971, that's 400 years.

SOUTH AMERICA

― Atacama Desert

■ Chile

The amount of water on Earth never changes but it can exist as a liquid, a solid (ice) or a gas (**water vapour**).

# THE POTATO FAMINE IN IRELAND

**Peasants** in Ireland worked for the landowners and gave their crops to their **landlords** as rent. They had very little land to provide food for themselves, so they grew potatoes, which give a good **yield**. Potatoes fill you up and are nutritious. For these reasons, the potato was vital for the survival of Irish peasants. Suddenly, in September 1845, disaster struck, as a fungus-like disease attacked the crop.

## MOST SERIOUSLY AFFECTED COUNTIES

1. Galway
2. Mayo
3. Sligo
4. Roscommon
5. Leitrim
6. Cavan

## BADLY AFFECTED COUNTIES

1. Longford
2. Westmeath
3. Clare
4. Tipperary
5. Laois
6. Waterford
7. Cork
8. Kerry

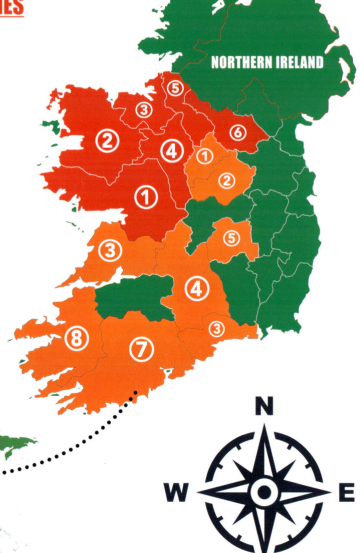

10

The disease was called potato blight and had been transported in ships sailing from North America. Within a few days, it had killed the entire crop, turning the potatoes black and mushy. The only crops left belonged to the landlords and were sold in Great Britain. Thousands of Irish peasants starved in what became known as The Potato Famine.

**Irish peasants starving during The Potato Famine.**

In the towns, people fought with soldiers to try to stop food being **exported**. As a result, new laws were passed, encouraging landlords to tumble – knock down – the peasants' homes. In the years that followed, many people left Ireland, bound for Canada, Australia, the United Kingdom and the USA. Many more could not afford to travel so they sold everything they owned and tried to survive by eating nettles and weeds.

**A priest blesses kneeling peasants as they try to leave Ireland.**

**Between 1845 and 1855, one and a half million people left Ireland for the USA.**

The British government made the problem worse by not stopping the export of food out of Ireland. Eventually, grain was sent to Ireland, but it was too expensive for the starving peasants to buy and was of poor quality. Sir Charles Trevelyan, an important British lord, called the famine "the judgement of God". He and many educated Britons believed the Irish peasants had brought the problems on themselves.

**A monument in West Ireland for the victims who wandered through this area looking for food.**

# THE GREAT PLAINS DROUGHT IN THE USA

The Great Plains is a vast area of farmland in the USA, which is mostly used for growing wheat. It stretches as far south as Texas and almost as far north as Canada. For many years, the combination of rich soil and plenty of rain produced good crops but, at the beginning of the 1930's, there was little to no rainfall. Temperatures soared while crops withered and died.

**The labelled states were all affected by the drought. The area that was the most seriously affected, in the centre of Colorado, Kansas, Oklahoma, Texas and New Mexico, became known as The Dust Bowl.**

① Montana
② North Dakota
③ South Dakota
④ Wyoming
⑤ Nebraska
⑥ Colorado
⑦ Kansas
⑧ Oklahoma
⑨ Texas
⑩ New Mexico
⑪ California

U.S.A.

CANADA

MEXICO

GULF OF MEXICO

ATLANTIC OCEAN

PACIFIC OCEAN

The topsoil that plants grow in takes thousands of years to develop. In the dry conditions, however, it turned to dust and blew away in minutes in the high winds. Dust storms, called black blizzards, blotted out the Sun. The worst dust storms happened on 14 April 1935, when, it was reported, you could not see your hand in front of your face. Nothing grew and farmers faced ruin as their crops and animals died.

**The colour of the dust showed where the storm came from – black from Kansas, red from Oklahoma and grey from Colorado.**

**Black dust clouds over Texas in 1936.**

**Machinery and a barn buried by dust in South Dakota in 1936.**

Some people left, many for California, but three quarters of the **Dust Bowlers** remained, living very difficult lives.

People leaving for California – they became known as "Okies" because so many were from Oklahoma.

People tried to protect themselves by taking refuge in **tornado** shelters and cellars. They hung wet sheets across doorways and over beds, to try to trap the dust, but it caused deaths and illness in people and livestock.

Lung damage caused by the dust was called "dust pneumonia".

Unemployed farmers in Texas.

Although lack of rain caused the drought, the problems were made worse because the land had been farmed too much. Grasses and shrubs that once held the soil together had been removed to give more space for farm land. In 1936, a man called Hugh Bennett persuaded the government to pay farmers to farm in better ways, for example by replanting grasslands. Finally, in Autumn 1939, it rained and the area came back to life.

**Crops and animals are once again flourishing on The Great Plains.**

# FAMINE AND
# DROUGHT IN ETHIOPIA

Ethiopia, in Eastern Africa, is a country where many people live in poverty. Farming and **agriculture** are very important as they provide over three quarters of the jobs and nearly two thirds of the country's exports. Record low rainfall in the mid-1980s was, therefore, a very serious problem. Five areas – Gojjam, Eritrea, Hararghe, Tigray and Wollo – were particularly affected by the lack of rain. Ethiopia has suffered many droughts in its history but this one was to be a **catastrophe**.

① **Gojjam**
② **Eritrea**
(now a separate country)
③ **Hararghe**
④ **Tigray**
⑤ **Wollo**

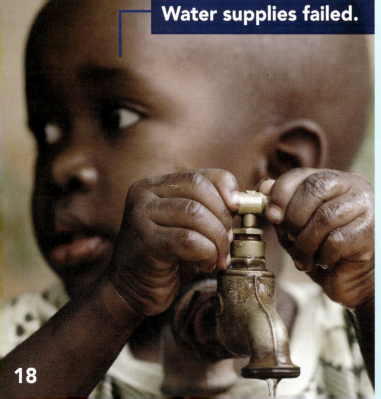

**Water supplies failed.**

As crops and animals died, food became more and more **scarce**, so prices started to rise. Poor peasant farmers could not afford to eat and began to starve. They had always lived from **harvest** to harvest and had never been able to store any food to protect themselves against crop failures. Any spare food had always been taken and sold by the landowners. Now, a deadly famine took hold.

View of drought-hit farmland in Ethiopia, taken from the air.

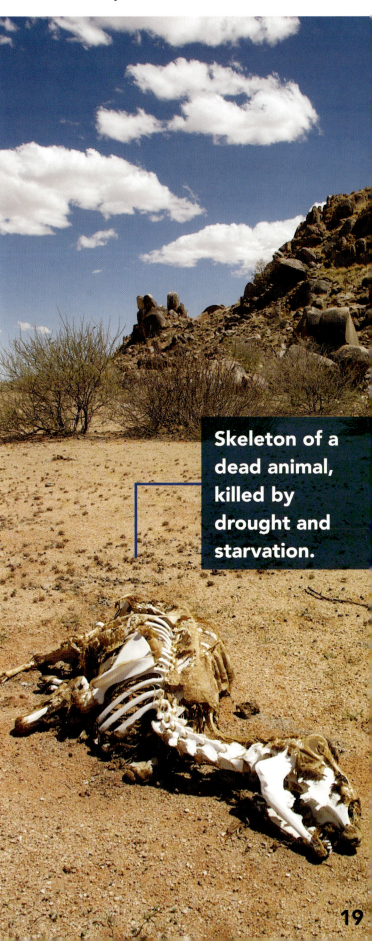

Skeleton of a dead animal, killed by drought and starvation.

On 23 October 1984, a television **journalist** called Michael Buerk reported on the crisis from a **refugee** camp in Korem, Ethiopia. He described the place as "the closest thing to Hell on Earth". His report attracted the attention of people all around the world. A famous singer, Sir Bob Geldof, assembled a group of other singers called Band Aid. In December 1984, they released a track called "Do They Know It's Christmas?", which raised millions of pounds to help the people of Ethiopia.

Sir Bob Geldof

The Live Aid concert, also organised by Sir Bob Geldof, was held in two places at the same time, Wembley Stadium in London and the John F Kennedy Stadium in Philadelphia. It too raised millions of pounds.

Fighting prevented food from being transported to where it was needed.

The drought was not the only problem that caused the famine in Ethiopia. Many years of **civil war** and protests against the government had made the country weak and unable to deal with the crisis.

The government also tried to force people to move south to unaffected areas, but failed to provide the things they had promised, like housing. People could not settle and food production decreased further.

Today, Ethiopia still suffers droughts but foreign aid has helped to ensure that food can be moved to the people who need it.

Teff is an important food crop in Ethiopia.

# THE BIG DRY

For many Australians, drought is accepted as part of their lives. In 2003, however, a drought which began in 1995 was recognised as the worst in the country's history. It continued in many areas until 2012 and some regions are still affected. Known as The Big Dry, it caused difficulties for many people. but is an example of how drought does not necessarily lead to famine.

**Did you know? On average, people in Australia use over three times more water each day than people in the UK.**

① Perth
② Melbourne
③ Adelaide
④ Brisbane
⑤ Sydney
⑥ Hobart
⑦ Canberra

**Queensland, Victoria and Western Australia were the worst affected but the drought also hit parts of South Australia, New South Wales and Tasmania.**

Lakes and rivers dried up and the production of important crops like cotton and rice was affected. Many jobs in **tourism** and farming were lost. As grasslands died and animal food became scarce and expensive, farmers struggled to feed their livestock. In 2009, serious bush fires, brought on by drought conditions, high winds and soaring temperatures, struck the state of Victoria.

**The worst day of fires, 7th February 2009, became known as Black Saturday.**

Fire crews struggled to stop the fires spreading.

Signs like these warned people of the dangers.

The **recycling** of waste water means that you could be drinking water that has been in your bath or washing machine! Of course, it has been cleaned first! At the time of The Big Dry, many countries, for example the United Kingdom and the USA, had been recycling waste water for some time. It was not until 2007, however, that severe drought conditions forced the introduction of recycling centres in Australia.

Severe drought conditions like this have led to water-saving measures like recycling.

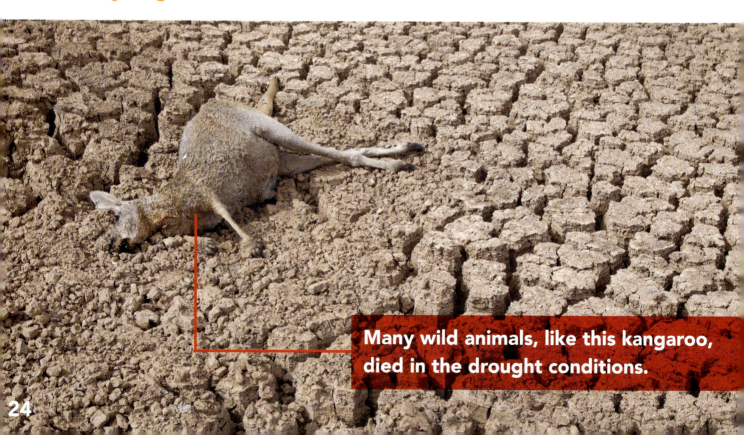

Many wild animals, like this kangaroo, died in the drought conditions.

Water tanks like this save precious rainfall.

Many plans have been introduced to save water. In some states, residents are given rebates – money off their water bills – if they do things to help them use less water. These include fitting tanks which collect rainfall, swimming pool covers that stop evaporation and washing machines, taps and shower heads that use only tiny amounts of water. Other ideas include building desalination plants, which remove salt from sea water so that it is safe to drink.

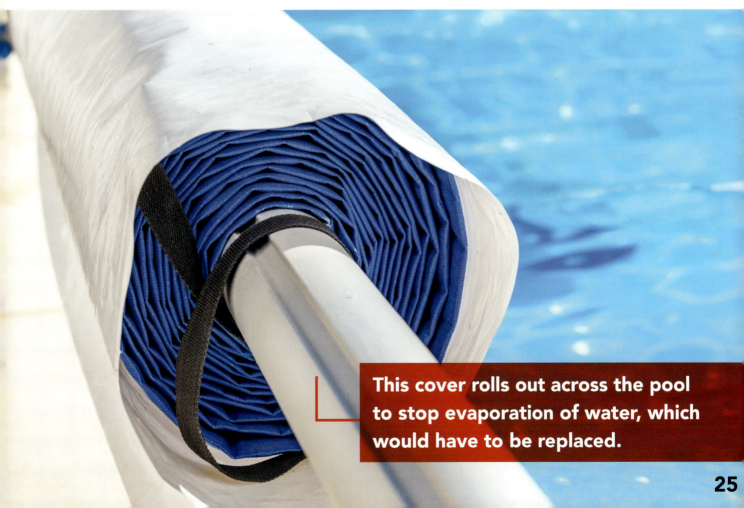

This cover rolls out across the pool to stop evaporation of water, which would have to be replaced.

25

# GLOBAL WARMING

Every day, people around the world burn **fossil fuels** to run their cars and to provide electricity for homes and businesses. As they burn, fossil fuels release carbon dioxide and methane, which are known as **greenhouse gases**. These form an invisible layer around the Earth. Heat from the Sun passes through, but at night, some of this heat is trapped by greenhouse gases and cannot escape back into space. Scientists think that this process is slowly heating up our planet. They call this effect global warming.

Have you ever stood inside a hot greenhouse on a sunny day? Greenhouse gases absorb heat in the same way as the air in a greenhouse.

Fumes from power stations and car exhaust emissions contain greenhouse gases.

In some parts of the world, global warming will cause severe flooding as sea levels rise. In areas where drought is already common, however, **heatwaves** are expected to last longer and be hotter than previously experienced. Millions of people could be affected by lack of food and water. Already, about seventeen in every twenty people live in the driest parts of our planet.

**The Chacaltaya glacier in Bolivia, South America provided water for drinking and irrigation. Global warming has melted the glacier, causing water shortages in the region.**

SOUTH AMERICA

① Bolivia

**Around the world, about 315,000 children a year are killed by diseases caused by unclean water.**

① La Paz
△ Chacaltaya

N
W E
S

# WHAT CAN W

*Reduce greenhouse gases by using less energy* – Switch off TVs, lights and computers. Dry clothes outside. Walk to school. Buy locally grown food, as less energy is needed to store and transport it. You can check where your food has come from by looking at the label on the product.

*Save water* – Use a bucket, not a hose pipe, to wash the car. A shower uses much less water than a bath. Switch off the tap while you clean your teeth.

All the products in our homes need energy to produce them. Help to reduce greenhouse gases – reuse and recycle things at home, for example food packaging.

Support international charities. Visit www.wateraid.org and www.oxfam.org to find out how they are helping people around the world who are facing drought and famine.

28

# DO TO HELP?

## GOVERNMENTS CAN:

Encourage the building of eco-homes, which burn no fossil fuels and release no greenhouse gases.

Ensure that the food the world produces is shared out fairly. We already grow enough food to feed everyone.

Encourage the use of **renewable** forms of energy, like solar, wind, tidal and biomass, so that less fossil fuels are burned. Biomass energy is made by recycling plant and animal waste.

Prevent **de-forestation**. Trees help to remove the greenhouse gas carbon dioxide from the atmosphere.

# LOOKING TO THE FUTURE

The World Meteorological Organisation, a group of people who study the Earth's weather, tries to give advance warnings of natural disasters like droughts, so that governments can plan ahead. The population of the world is thought to be growing by fourteen people every minute, so demand for water will continue to grow. Many people will become **environmental refugees**, as growing desert areas force them to move elsewhere to find water.

In the past, most wars have been about land or oil. In the future, they are likely to be about fresh water.

Scientists are working on special crops, called genetically modified (GM) crops, which produce more food and are able to deal with pests and drought better than normal crops.

# GLOSSARY

| | |
|---|---|
| **agriculture** | growing crops |
| **catastrophe** | an extreme disaster |
| **cholera** | a serious and often deadly disease which causes sickness and diarrhoea |
| **civil war** | fighting between different groups of people in the same country |
| **currents** | steady flows of water in one direction |
| **deforestation** | the cutting down and removal of trees in a forest |
| **Dust Bowlers** | people who lived in The Dust Bowl during The Great Plains Drought |
| **environmental refugees** | people who have been forced to leave their homes because of natural dangers and disasters, for example a drought |
| **evaporate** | turn to vapour (gas), dry up |
| **exported** | sent to another country for sale |
| **finite** | having a limit or an end |
| **flash floods** | floods caused by sudden, heavy rain |
| **fossil fuels** | fuels such as coal, oil and gas, formed millions of years ago from the remains of animals and plants |
| **glaciers** | slowly moving masses of ice |
| **government** | the group of people in charge of a country or district |
| **greenhouse gases** | gases in the atmosphere that trap the Sun's heat |
| **harvest** | food gathered from crops at the end of the growing season |
| **heatwaves** | spells of particularly hot weather |
| **ice caps** | areas with a covering of ice that never melts |
| **irrigation** | man- made systems that add water to crops to help them grow |
| **journalist** | someone who reports for a newspaper or TV channel |
| **landlords** | people who rent out land or buildings for money |
| **nutrients** | substances that are required for healthy growth |
| **peasants** | poor land workers who do not own their own land |
| **pests** | destructive insects or animals which attack and damage crops or livestock |
| **recycling** | using something again |
| **refugee** | someone who has been forced to leave their home to escape danger |
| **renewable** | able to be replaced |
| **resource** | something that is of use or value |
| **scarce** | in short supply, hard to find |
| **starvation** | suffering or death, caused by lack of food |
| **tornado** | a fast-moving, strong and destructive wind, which forms into a funnel shape |
| **tourism** | travelling to a place for pleasure |
| **water vapour** | water in the form of a gas, but below boiling temperature |
| **wither** | become dried up, due to lack of water |
| **yield** | the amount of a crop that is produced |

# INDEX